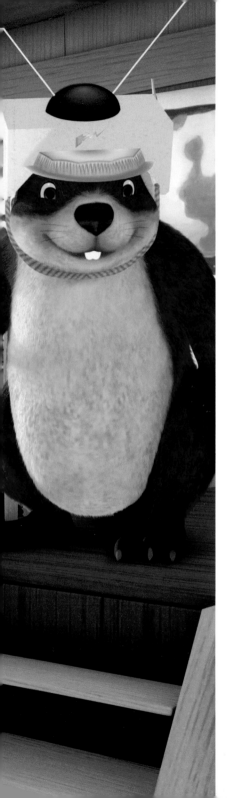

FRANKLIN and his friends had great imaginations. One day, they decided to play astronauts. They dressed up in special space gear and pretended their tree fort was a spaceship.

As they were getting ready to blast off into outer space, Franklin suddenly noticed someone was missing.

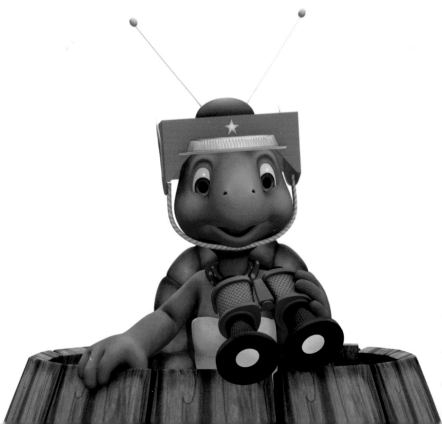

"Hold on, everybody!" yelled Franklin. "We forgot about Snail."
Franklin spotted Snail playing his harmonica outside of their tree fort.
"Hey, Snail," said Franklin. "Our spaceship is about to take off.
Climb aboard!"

"Thanks, Franklin," said Snail, "but I'm busy right now. I'm trying to play a song on my harmonica. It goes like this —"

"You can do that later," said Franklin. "We're taking off for Planet Glorp. Come on!"

"Well, okay," said Snail. He slowly climbed aboard the spaceship.

"Welcome aboard, Snail," said Bear. "On this ship, I'm called Space Bear."

"I'm Moon Beamer," said Beaver.

"Flash Fox, at your service," said Fox.

"Goose the Glorp is my name," said Goose.
"Planet Hopper here," said Rabbit.
"And I'm Captain Star," said Franklin.

Snail looked at his space friends. "That's neat. Who can I be?"

"You can be Robot," said Franklin. "All spaceships need a robot."

"Robot?" said Snail, frowning. "Do I have to be a robot?"

"Yes, and here's your space suit," said Franklin, wrapping him in tinfoil.

"I'd rather practice my new harmonica song," said Snail. "It goes like this —"

"You can do that later," said Franklin. "Your job is to sound the alarm in an emergency. Now let's blast off!"

Franklin and the rest of the crew got ready for takeoff.

"Five, four, three, two, one — blast off!" said Franklin.

Fox and Bear made sounds like an engine. Beaver and Goose shook back and forth in their seats.

Rabbit checked the instrument panel and said, "We are now in outer space!"

Everyone cheered.

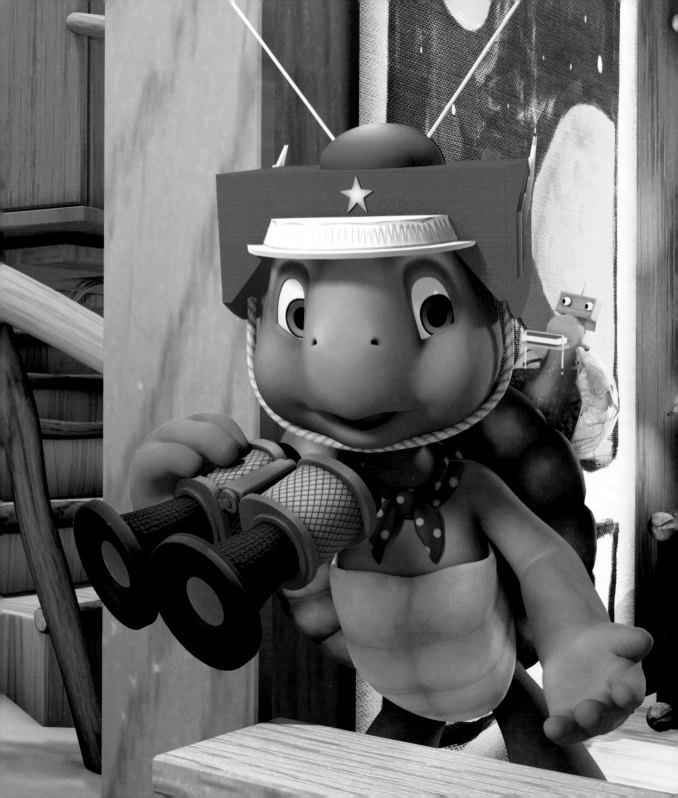

"Isn't it cool-io in outer space?" asked Franklin.

"Yes, it is," said Snail. "It makes me want to play a song. It goes like this —"

"You can do that later," said Franklin. "Right now, we have to avoid some giant meteors!"

Franklin accidentally bumped Snail and knocked his harmonica out the spaceship window.

"Oh, no! My harmonica!" said Snail.

"We can get it later," said Franklin. "I need you to sound the emergency!"

"Red alert! Emergency! Danger! Danger!" yelled Snail.

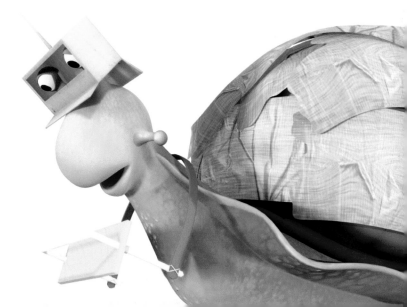

"What's the emergency?" asked Beaver.
"We're going to hit some meteors!" said Franklin.
"What are meteors?" asked Goose.

"They're like giant flying space rocks," explained Franklin.
"What are we going to do?" asked Rabbit.
"Flash Fox! Space Bear! Put the space brakes on!" yelled Franklin.

The crew managed to stop their spaceship before they hit the meteors.

"Franklin, can I get my harmonica now that we've stopped?" asked Snail.

"You can do that later," said Franklin. "We still have an emergency!"

"What now?" asked Bear.

"We have to land on Planet Glorp," said Franklin, checking his space chart.

While everyone else ran back to their stations, Snail sighed and slowly crept away. He didn't want to play astronauts anymore.

Franklin and his crew prepared to land on Planet Glorp. Rabbit took the controls and set the spaceship down on land.

"A perfect touchdown!" said Beaver.

"Come on, crew," said Franklin. "Let's check out this planet."

Everyone was ready for action. That's when Franklin noticed that someone was missing.

"Hey, where's Robot Snail?" asked Franklin. They searched the spaceship, but Snail was nowhere to be found.

"He must have gone down to Planet Glorp," said Franklin.
"Why would he do that?" asked Bear.
"I don't know," said Franklin.
"We have to save him," said Goose.
Together, the crew climbed out of the spaceship.

They searched everywhere, but there was no sign of Snail. Then they heard the sound of a harmonica.

"Did you hear that?" asked Franklin. "Come on!"

The friends followed the sound and found Snail in a hollow tree trunk.

"Snail, we were looking all over for you," said Franklin. "Why did you leave?"

"I wanted to play my harmonica, but you wouldn't let me."

"I just wanted you to have fun with us," said Franklin.

"I like playing with you guys, but I also like playing my harmonica," said Snail. "It's fun, too."

"Sorry, Snail," said Franklin. "I guess I didn't think about that. But if you give us another chance, I think I know a way we all can have fun."

"Okay, Franklin," said Snail.

The crew returned to the spaceship. As Snail played his harmonica,
Franklin and his friends sang:
"Blast off! Blast off! Here goes our spaceship!
Blast off! Blast off! For a super space trip!
We'll zoom past the stars, through a comet's tail!
We're on a space adventure with our friend Robot Snail!"

Franklin's Spaceship

Kids Can Press